Nora Sänger

BONFIRES

music & novelette

Bibliografische Information der Deutschen Nationalbibliothek: Die Deutsche Nationalbibliothek verzeichnet diese Publikation in der Deutschen Nationalbibliografie; detaillierte bibliografische Daten sind im Internet über http://dnb.dnb.de abrufbar.

Lektorat: Anneken Hertzler
Covergestaltung: Jessica Stute
Coverbild: Linda Nonnewitz „Streets", Acryl auf Leinwand

Verlag: BoD · Books on Demand GmbH, Überseering 33, 22297 Hamburg, bod@bod.de

Druck: Libri Plureos GmbH, Friedensallee 273, 22763 Hamburg

ISBN: 978-3-7693-2346-7

BONFIRES

CREDITS

lyrics: Nora Sänger
music: Nora Sänger, Stefan Rebelski

produced and
arranged by Stefan Rebelski
Instagram: stefanrebelski_keys

electric guitar: Eike Ernst
Instagram: eikeernstrings

pedal steel: Nils Tuxen

all vocals: Nora Sänger

cover photography: Sandra Wiering
Instagram: sandrawiering

get „Bonfires" and „Bonfires (acoustic)" here:

norasanger.bandcamp.com

BONFIRES
acoustic

the smell in the air
takes me back
to where you last took my
hand
and we were just there
fully absorbed
and enjoying the moment
Bonfires everywhere…

something in the air
I knew it then
and I know it now, somehow
that feeling was rare
no hidden agenda
no motifs
just love, I vow
Bonfires everywhere…

and now I'm driving down
Sycamore Lane
I can feel you whisper
calling out my name
come into my arms again
Bonfires everywhere…

I'm out of the blue
I never followed those invites
but now I am after you
how pathetic am I !?
what a mess
did I really think I'd get away
with this?
my life's a lie …
I lie, baby, who am I ?

and I'm breathing in
this smoky memory

and it is as though
this long lost girl is
waving at me
(rekindeling a spark in me)

and old flame never dies
can I even look in your eyes?
after bailing on you
cavin' in to family lies
this old flame never died
I'm begging you!
they say first love, last love…

I'm praying you're there alone
my heart couldn't bear
you taking someone else
home
ain't I better than them?
those simple small-town bit-
ches?
all they got are hacks
for thermomixes!

but even now
I still feel you were my home
who am I kidding
I have no sense of home…
could I ever be your home!?

and old flame never dies
can I even look into your
eyes?
after bailing on you
cavin' in to family lies
this old flame never died
I'm begging you!
they say first love, last love

yeah you're my first love, last
love

I am aware that the term 'Bonfire Night' refers to Guy Fawkes Night
on November 5.
After some consideration I took it for the fictional tradition in this
story. The story was inspired by a song I wrote, *Bonfires*, which itself
was inspired by the German tradition of Easter Bonfire (Osterfeuer).
I would imagine it is well possible that a few small towns in rural
Kentucky could have their own
Bonfire Night tradition apart from Guy Fawkes Night in the UK.
So I have humbly borrowed the term for this story.

"Don't touch!" said the note that Darren had posted to the bottle of rosé in the fridge. With an exclamation mark. Yelling it at her as if she didn't already walk on eggshells around his hundred-dollar wines. Any other night she would have accepted this move, justifying it in regards to the price of the bottle or the passion that Darren had for wines. But tonight, after being groped at the office by Stanford, which had totally crossed the line — it was too much. And everything that she normally kept at a distance came tumbling down on her.

The dark circles under her eyes from countless all-nighters, even though she was far enough up the rank to dump doc reviews on someone else. But she just couldn't.

The wine tastings with her and Darren's wine club when her facial muscles would hurt from smiling.

His migraines that would save her from having to sleep with him.

Stanford's flabby boner in her mouth, nauseating her, his hands in her hair ruining her updo, her shutting herself off against what he'd say, his smell, his taste, everything.

And it seemed like the silver lining, the promise, the way out, was all there in that one Facebook push notification *Bonfire Night* that had appeared on her cell the moment before she had opened the fridge. Tonight was Bonfire Night. It was her hometown Mayer's Creek's beloved annual social event and there was a good chance that Chris Jacobs would be there.

She tiptoed into her walk-in closet, and shut the door. *What kind of life have I made for myself?* She went through her uniformed pant suits and leisure wear, but all her blouses and cashmere cardigans were too stuck up for Bonfire Night, even she knew that, and deep in her heart she had known what she wanted to wear right when she recalled Stanford's greedy hand on her backside. And that was Chris' old lumberjack shirt, a blue and cream plaid, which Chris had once lent her and she had ended up taking with her to Durham all those years ago. She had cherished it as a pledge ever since, and maybe, just maybe, tonight was the night for it to be redeemed. The thought alone made her feel faint. If nothing else, she had something cool to wear for the occasion. Something that would communicate *I belong here* or, more accurately: *I belonged here.*

Slipping into the shirt felt exciting in a daring, somewhat forbidden way, and she felt funny looking into the mirror. Like, this wasn't her but it was. Hopefully it was.

She sneaked by Darren's office, he was sitting at the computer like always. In about an hour and a half he would appear expecting a dinner scenario involving maybe pasta, or fish, or both, and that damned bottle of rosé.

In one fluid movement she grabbed her black puffer coat, her keys and wallet, and exited the apartment without making a sound. Running down the stairs, yes, she was racing down and for some reason not taking the elevator like always, she realized she still had her hair pinned up. Quickly she took out the pins and ruffled through the loose hair with her hands. It felt like the first time in years she that she had truly noticed her hair. Apparently she hadn't paid much attention to her light brown, soft curls ever since she started only wearing them up, because the length of them surprised her now.

She got in her car, fastened the seatbelt, and started the engine decidedly. She sped out of the garage heading for Highway 71, crossing the Ohio River into Kentucky.

When the concrete buildings bit by bit made room for trees and meadows, she rolled her window down. A chilly breeze surrounded her, lifting up her hair and tickling her face. She inhaled that breeze somewhat meditatively, closing her eyes for a second. A smile flickered in the corner of her mouth but the next moment she felt stupid. Was she really about to intrude there, barge in on that familiarity? Wasn't it presumptuous to think she was still welcome there, following the Facebook invite only now, after so many years of receiving and never responding to it? *Kinda self-involved, actually*, she thought. *All of a sudden this chick that we barely remember, who left here for a career in law in order to become filthy rich, appears.* Alienated, aloof. Ashamed.

It was a two hour drive to Mayer's Creek. Plenty of time to change her mind and turn around.

Chris Jacobs. She wondered what he'd look like now, if he still spoke in that deep, calm and soothing tone that would turn raspy when he was mad but trying to hold it back.

Twenty-two years, she thought. Twenty-two years ago she climbed in the back of his truck with him to chat awkwardly, naively and magically, looking at the bonfire out on the field and the people gathering around it, ashes rising in the air, the scent of smoke giving it an almost sacred vibe. And he clumsily took her hand and she let him: she had hoped something of the kind would happen for about half a year. He had asked her to dance with him at Homecoming and she had, even though she'd thought they didn't really fit. She had hung out with the popular people and he hadn't. But it had been just one dance, she could grant him that.

The song they'd danced to was 'Wonderwall' by Oasis, and he'd told her that he had seen them play in Atlanta that year in the summer. He had driven down with his Dad and it had been a really great show and he liked their music a lot. He'd said that ,Wonderwall' was one of these songs that made him wanna just lay in the back of his truck and look up into the stars. "Cheesy, right?" he'd said shyly, but then she'd stepped on his foot which had completely embarrassed her. He'd said "Thank you, that really sets this dance apart from the other ones" and he'd chuckled and she couldn't help but giggle as well. And then the song'd been over and he'd tipped his imaginary hat to her and had said "Miss" and was gone. She'd looked after him, enchanted, and had gone back over to Stella Hancock, her best friend then. "How was it?" Stella had asked and she had shrugged and said "alright". But the following weeks she had found herself peeking at him during lunch, checking him out and thinking of him. Of his monologue about Oasis and their music. She'd never seen meaning in music like that. To add to it he'd been very cute, wearing his dark waves in a messy bob, combining lumberjack shirts with skater jeans and having the most amazing smile, whimsical and warm.

She'd worried about how she could pull off hanging out with someone who was not a straight A student or in the Honor Society or a sports ace. Chris hadn't been completely unpopular, he was on the basketball team even, not a top player but a solid one. So that'd been something. If she'd been on some imaginary A-list at her high school, he'd been B. B-listers were close enough to the A-group to talk to and hang out with. But independent enough to be up for stuff that would have been too damaging for a common A-lister's image, she would find out.

She tore herself away from these golden memories by thinking *he's probably with someone anyway. He most likely tied the knot with that bitch Leslie Smitts.* That had been one of the last pieces of news to reach her in Durham. Stella Hancock had gotten it from Renee Harrison, that Chris Jacobs and Leslie Smitts were dating. So there was a fair chance that it was still on.

Bonfire Night was a thing in Mayer's Creek and a few more towns close by. People told each other that this local custom had been brought over by German immigrants who would hold bonfires the night before Easter. It was a tradition that was supposed to see winter off and welcome spring. Wherever it came from, she had known and cherished it throughout her childhood and teenage years. As a kid she would go to Mayer's fairgrounds, the field where Bonfire Night was held, with her parents and her brother. Snacking corn dogs and sipping sodas, she'd play with other kids, trying to throw sticks into the fire or dancing around in front of the small stage where a local band would play. As a teenager, she would meet her friends there. And even though at around fifteen she and Stella would start telling each other that the event was square and dull with only a bunch of hillbillies going there, they'd still go, because they had grown up with it and it was part of them in a way that they couldn't get rid of. Also because it'd been a good opportunity to sneak a sip of beer or bourbon from someone who hid some in their truck.

And once she was with Chris, Bonfire Night would be the most magical thing to her anyway, because that's where he'd first taken her hand. And because he'd been able to enjoy himself there apart from concepts or agendas and she'd admired that in him.

She saw two columns of smoke rise into the sky when she drove through Mayer's Creek's neighbouring towns. Bonfires everywhere, it seemed. Excitement rose in her but took a hit when her phone rang. Darren, for the fifth time. She ignored him for the fifth time. Just like the calls and messages from Stanford and her assistant Mia that had reached her since she left

17

Cincinnati. They could all leave her the hell alone. She had played their games long enough and most likely would go back to doing so the next day anyways. Or not? She felt butterflies in her stomach as she fleetingly considered the idea of playing hooky. Playing hooky in the arms of Chris Jacobs.

She couldn't help but scoff at herself for this. Yet, wasn't this why she was going?

The roadside was lined with cars, mostly trucks, which made her Mercedes stand out. She parked and turned off the engine.

As she got out of her car, she looked over to the field where a huge stack of branches slowly burned. She was too far away to recognize anyone. All she saw were silhouettes in front of the flickering flames. It made her smile.

She had made it. She hadn't backed out. She was really here.

She tried to study the silhouettes from where she stood. How many of them would she know? For a moment, she drifted off into mental images of reuniting with the people from her high school class, smiling, hugging, being welcomed back. The prodigal daughter, finally home. And the crowd of friends would split and Chris Jacobs would emerge, coming towards her, wrapping her in his arms, solving it all for her.

Pull yourself together already.

She waited for a moment.

What was she thinking? It hit her only now that she might only run into old neighbors, or former friends of her parents, who had themselves turned their backs on this place just like she had. Why would the left-behinds save her spot? A spot she had never seemed to care for while she held it, worse even, kicked with her feet. Suddenly the evening seemed a lot more likely to end up with her getting cornered and interrogated.

This was ridiculous. She was ridiculous. She took out her phone.

There were several messages from Darren and a few from Stanford. She wouldn't touch Stanfords messages with a ten-foot pole after what had gone down at the office earlier that day.

She'd made a quick stop at the coffee machine in order to stretch her legs for once, busy getting back to her paperwork, and the idiot had come after her, squeezing her butt while she'd waited for the espresso to run though. "When will I see you again?" he had said under his breath while his sweaty hand rubbed over her pencil skirt. But then the sound of approaching footsteps had made him jerk himself away towards the fridge, opening it as if he'd been looking for something. Mortified, she had taken her espresso, fighting back tears on the way back to her office.

She read Darren's messages instead: "Weren't you gonna be home tonight?" "Call me." "What's the plan?"

No, dining at home with Darren, exchanging reports from work, listening to him make smart-ass remarks about that rosé still didn't sound like an appealing prospect for the night. Until now she had seen his obsession with picking the right wines as a sign of impeccable taste; had thought it was one of the things that made him a great, educated, socially intelligent man. However, now she was wrapped in the lumberjack shirt. Now she was overlooking the rustic loveliness that Bonfire Night was to her. And she found Darren's wine compulsion phony, like, it's a drink for crying out loud, either grape will make you dizzy in the head. She started typing: "Something's come up at work. I'll be home late. Got you the red snapper you asked for. In the fridge. Should go nicely with the Zinfandel. Don't wait for me." She hit 'send', looked up and put her phone in the pocket of her coat. She took a deep breath of smokey air and started walking towards the fire.

She couldn't even look at people. Sure, she wanted to find out who was there, but the thought of being discovered made her anxious. She couldn't bring herself to make eye contact with anyone. She meandered randomly through the crowd for a while, keeping her sight detached which made her feel as though she was drunk. A drink, there was a thought. She steered towards a booth. A big glass of white wine was exactly what she needed right now.

"What can I do for you, young lady?" said the white haired guy with a trucker hat and a bushy mustache behind the bar.

Wyatt from the liquor store. He looked at her and she got the feeling that he was trying to make out who she was. But he didn't say a thing.

"A white wine, please."

"White wine?" He chuckled a bit. "I can get you a beer, a bourbon, or a soda."

"A bourbon and coke then." *Yuck.*

She took a big sip and then another one. Then she decided that if she was going down that road she could as well go all the way, and so she went for the other booth where they sold greasy, carbs-laden corn dogs. Just as she took the first bite, somebody said "Jenna?".

She turned around and found herself face to face with a woman. At first glance the woman looked a few years older than herself. But then she noticed her unnaturally tanned complexion and the lines that show when you visit the tanning studio a little too frequently. She realized that the woman was not at all older than her and that it was in fact Leslie Smitts, of all people.

"What are you doing here?" Leslie asked and added, "I mean, it's been forever since we've last seen you around."

She panicked, said "Mmmh!" and pointed to her chewing mouth to stall. She chewed. Chewed more. Attempted to collect herself. Swallowed dramatically. Cleared her throat and went: "Leslie, hi. Good to see you."

"So odd that you're here."

"Yeah, right? I was... I was over in Louisville at my parents'. The fact that it was Bonfire Night came up as we talked and I, I thought I'd... have a look. Have a corn dog." She held up her corn dog, and tried a conversational laugh. "Before heading back home."

"Wow", said Leslie. "Your parents are in Louisville. And where are you?"

"Cincinatti."

"Alright, Cincy, nice."

"Yeah, it's great there. Really a great city to live in."

"Oh I bet. So, who else have you met here so far?"

"Oh, you're the first one. I was really hungry."

"For sure, for sure... Betty's corn dogs are the best."

"Absolutely."

They exchanged a few more inanities. Leslie looked at her with a pleasant smile that seemed to Jenna like a poker face. Leslie most likely spied her out, checking to see if she meant any danger.

"Are you here by yourself?" Jenna finally dared to ask, knowing what kind of statement she could provoke with such a question. Something that would include the phrase 'Chris and I'. She braced herself and Leslie pointed to a group in a little distance. "No, of course not, we're here with our friends. I just spotted you when I was going to get a beer."

Jenna looked at their friends, but she couldn't make out anybody she knew. Chris wasn't there. But that didn't mean anything, maybe he was getting something from the car or was using the bathroom. These were *their* friends. How wonderful to get a reality check after only fifteen minutes.

"Do you wanna come over with me and say hi to everyone?" Leslie offered. *No thank you*, Jenna thought. She didn't come here to see Leslie and Chris play happy couple in front of her very eyes. But she could easily believe that Leslie would want to parade her life with Chris, because it meant that Leslie had won.

"That's kind of you but I think I'll mingle first."

Leslie nodded. "For sure. See you later then."

"Yeah."

She turned away from Leslie, tore off a bite from her corn dog and swallowed hard to make the lump in her throat go away.

She reached for her phone. And then, without looking at what he had texted, Jenna typed "Do you wanna go over Jarbers tomorrow?"

She returned to pacing by the side of the crowd. Her phone beeped, Stanford had gotten back to her immediately. *Shit.* "I'm bringing sushi. Noon?"

"Sounds great."

She should leave it at that. Get back into her car, wait for the bourbon and coke buzz to wear off and go back. Save herself from the humiliation of a happily married Chris Jacobs realizing she, pathetic and sad, still hungered for him. The push notification for Bonfire Night confused her every year, she was used to that. This year it had really kicked in apparently. People get confused all the time. Why shouldn't she. There was no shame in admitting she had been wrong about driving here, right?

She put her phone back in her pocket, emptied her cup and looked up decidedly. And that was when her gaze fell on Mary Henderson. Yeah. It was her.

Jenna turned to the direction of her car, but found herself hesitating; looked back over to Mary, who stood by the fire with some friends. *Damn it*, she thought, and went over to her.

Mary was engaged in a conversation, so Jenna waited for her to finish a sentence before she lightly put her hand on Mary's shoulder to get her attention. "Hi Mary," she said.

Mary turned to her. It took her a second to know who stood in front of her. Her eyes lit up. "Oh my gosh, Jenna!" she exclaimed surprisedly, and instantly gave her a huge hug. Jenna struggled to go along with that amount of effusiveness. However, that hug did come as a relief. Finally. An argument tipping the scale in favor of her being here.

"What on earth are you doing here!?" Mary asked.

"I, I... spur of the moment decision. I realized it was Bonfire Night and I drove out. Just like that."

"That's awesome, it is so good seeing you!" Mary beamed. "Here, you remember Kevin Goldman. He's my husband."

"Sure, good to see you", she said and tried her best to hug Kevin Mary-style. And she did remember that Mary and Kevin had dated in high school. Small towns.

"Jenna Briggs, wow, it's been ages", Kevin said, "Good to have you back." And this was a lie, Jenna was sure, but it still did something for her that these people said these things.

Mary introduced her to the other two couples in the group: "Jenna and I graduated from LaSalle High together, we've been friends since elementary." *Until I traded you in for Stella Hancock when your ordinariness didn't do it for me anymore*, Jenna thought.

"That's a surprise", said one of the other women, "I've never heard of you."

"Oh, it's been a long time since I moved-"

"Jenna was set up for success early on" Mary told them. "She went to Duke and... became a lawyer!?" Mary looked at Jenna, smiling excitedly and Jenna nodded. "There you go", Mary proclaimed to her friends and Jenna felt like an unexpected winner at a beauty pageant. No one had betted on or wanted her yet still here she was. "I'm in corporate law", she said plainly.

"That's nice." Mary said. "And where do you live now?"

"Cincinnati."

"How lovely! Kevin and I just took the kids there three weeks ago to go shopping. Such a wonderful city. Are you familiar with Cincinnati Premium Outlets?"

"I've heard of it."

"I picked up a Michael Kors purse for only 49 bucks and Kyra found her prom dress - Saks Fifth Avenue!"

The others went "wow!" and Jenna tried an enthusiastic smile while calculating that Mary must have become a mom at twenty.

And so she hung around with Mary and her friends Nina and Beth, with their husbands standing next to them having their own conversation.

From time to time she looked around but never spotted Chris.

Beth went to get another round for them and Jenna sipped more bourbon and coke, which made it easier for her to relax and enjoy this.

Mary, Nina and Beth talked about the new minister at their church for a while who supposedly was more conservative than the last one so their teens couldn't connect to him that well. Beth asked her if she belonged to a church and she said "No."

"But Jenna's family did belong to All Saints back in the day", Mary told them. Then she said to Jenna: "Remember when we tried to wear matching clothes to Sunday school every darn Sunday?" and smiled. And Jenna needed a moment but then she did remember. "Oh, yeah... we always showed each other possible items to wear through our windows." Jenna smiled, too.

"We were next door neighbors", Mary told her friends, "and of course our parents weren't up to buying us the exact same things, but we would wear a shirt in the same color and then one of us a denim skirt and the other one denim pants."

"Oh that's adorable!" Nina said, "how old were you then?"

Jenna looked at Mary. "Maybe eleven, twelve?"

Mary nodded. "Yeah. We rode the bus to school together and sat next to each other in class." She paused for a moment as if to explore the memory. "But then in high school we ended up taking different classes. I mean, I was never as smart as Jenna." Mary shrugged but it didn't seem as though it bothered her. "So we sort of drifted apart towards the end of freshman year." It didn't sound like an accusation but still, it made Jenna wonder. *How could I ever leave her behind for fucking Stella Hancock with her conceit, her complicated clothing policies, her strategical socializing!?* It made her feel like she should apologize to Mary, but it was too early for drunken confessions. "We did sing karaoke together at the Prom after party though, remember?" Mary said and chuckled. How could Jenna forget. "Yeah, right, you and I sang Destiny's Child, right?"

"Tried to, you mean. 'Jumpin' Jumpin'" I believe it was."

Jenna laughed. "Oh my gosh."

"And then Kevin and Chris tried to beat us by singing 'Higher'... do you remember? I always hated that song."

Chris. She had said his name, just like that. Jenna swallowed. "Totally, the song sucked."

"But they did a better job than us", Mary pointed out.

"It's a way easier song. I mean, Destiny's Child. Beyoncé!"

"You're right. They just took the easy way out." They both laughed at the memory and Nina said "I can't believe Kevin would actually sing karaoke!" "Yeah, it was a long time ago", Mary replied, turned to Jenna and asked: "Have you ever heard from Chris again?"

"No", Jenna said trying to sound nonchalant.

"A Chris that we know?" Beth asked.

"Uhm, Jacobs", Mary told her.

"Oh really, you don't say", was Beth's reaction and Jenna couldn't help but read things into this. *You don't say.* That couldn't be a neutral comment. Had Beth been involved with Chris at some point? Was there something about her, Jenna, that made it hard to believe that she had once been his girlfriend? But at least she had certainty now that he was still around.

"Are you with someone now?" Nina interrupted her thoughts.

"Yeah. I have a boyfriend of four years, his name is Darren." Great. Jenna cursed herself. That could have been a window. But she closed it without even trying.

"Where is he now?"

"In Cincinnati. Working, probably."

"On a Saturday night. Is he, like, a cop or doctor?"

"No." All of a sudden, Jenna did feel embarrassed. "He's in finance, investments. We're real workaholics, the two of us." She stopped for a moment. Asked herself why she wavered. "I mean, me too, I should be going over a case right now... but I decided to take the night off." She tried not to sound too doubtful.

"Good for you!" Nina said and Mary joined in with an "Absolutely!"

Jenna gulped the rest of her bourbon and coke, wanting to swallow her uneasiness. But for what it was worth, at least it had taken the girls' attention away from Chris Jacobs.

Only for a few minutes though, it seemed. Because then, when Jenna let her gaze wander across the crowd, there he was. She squinted her eyes against the darkness and the flicker from the fire, but she knew it was him.

Her heart started pounding and then she felt a punch to her gut because of the two teenage boys by his side, the younger one being his spitting image.

How could she not have considered that he had kids?

Why had he had kids with anyone except her?

Fuck it, she didn't want kids.

What now?

And for about the millionth time since it happened, she was triggered into recalling the scenes of their breakup.

By the end of their junior year, she had gotten nervous. They had been dating for almost one and a half years when twelfth grade started, and even though Chris hadn't fit in perfectly with her chosen crowd, she'd held on to him dearly. He would laugh at her for not getting converse sneakers when she actually liked them just because Stella Hancock wouldn't approve of them. But he'd also get her dilemma and wrap her in his arms as if to shield her from those complicated agendas at least for a few minutes.

Chris came from a working-class family. His grandparents had sold the horse breeding operation that his family had run for generations in order to lessen their workload. His dad had started a plumbing business. But the family had kept two horses and Chris had loved them. He'd tried to get her into the whole equestrian thing, bringing her to the horses and making her climb on one of them with him and ride for a bit.

But she hadn't really warmed up to it. What she'd loved about being with the horses was watching Chris' passion.

Because that was something she'd never known, she now thought. Back in the day, she'd thought that being a top student was her passion. Academic achievements, medals and trophies, all the way from spelling bees to debate competitions and being a member of the National Honor Society. And the applause for all this from her parents, especially her mom. That'd been her reward, her assurance. Assurance that she could be what her parents had never been because of running merely a small insurance office. „Don't follow in your father's footsteps", her mom had said many times. „Go for finance. Or law."

Her parents had kept whatever they were thinking about Chris to themselves for a while. But when it had been time for Jenna to start thinking about college, the first questions had risen. „Does Chris plan on going to college?" „Does Chris have savings for college?" „Are Chris' basketball skills enough to get him a scholarship?" „What are Chris' career plans?"

Her own career plans had been law school since the tenth grade. She had taken her mom's words to heart when she'd seen that the fancy Stella Hancocks and Josh Fishers she hung out with had also considered law school the height of success. Her grades had been good enough, too. She had thought it a waste to not make use of them. So had the student counselor.

The phrase *college application* at the end of junior year had made her admit to herself that her plans would be difficult to combine with Chris'. "Make some money working for my dad first and then probably try and get a business degree at Northern Kentucky." *Damn him,* she'd thought. *How can he do that to me?* "Why don't you apply and start college and give it a chance? Maybe you'll like it", Jenna would try. But he would just say things like "Nah, I've hung around in class rooms enough for now, I need something else for a change. Work with my hands, make some money—" He'd smiled at her and added "Is that too tough on you?" and she had said "no!" quickly, trying to shush any inner turmoil.

Luckily, summer break had been around the corner. The perfect excuse to ignore her anxiousness for the time being. She'd spent as much time with Chris as she possibly could. He would pick her up in his truck and they'd drive... to the horses, to a lake, or to the mall. Sometimes they'd met his friends. It had shown that it was easier for the two of them to hang out with his friends than with hers. Of course, she hadn't found Sam and those guys agreeable. But she'd had to admit that it was fun to party with them occasionally. Agreeable or not, they were relaxed. And a part of her had secretly enjoyed those little breaks from her world.

If there'd been nothing else to do, she and Chris would simply drive around in his truck. Pull over somewhere, roll out that sleeping bag in the back and sleep together.

Sleeping with Chris under an open sky had been her favorite thing. She'd actually had orgasms then, unbelievable as it sounded to her now. It had been the best sex. No moves, no strategy, just holding on to each other. Saying *I love you* into each other's eyes. And meaning it. At least she had meant it. She liked to believe he'd meant it, too.

She had broken up with Chris three weeks before her move to Durham. After graduation, she'd taken on the task to ease him - and herself - into the idea of splitting up. There'd been no other option. Once or twice, she had secretly toyed around with the idea of asking him to come along to Durham. But something had told her that wasn't fitting for her. Even though it made her throat burn and her chest ache, she still went for it. Broke it to him, delivered all the arguments she had collected. At first, Chris had revolted against her, saying things like "that's bullshit" and "we can try it long distance." The case had been adjourned a couple of times - as planned by her - and after a few weeks of her reasoning with him, his resistance had melted and he'd seemed to understand that it was, in fact, better this way. His acceptance had devastated her.

So for the last three weeks before she'd started college, she'd hung out at home, depressed and heartbroken. Had let Stella Hancock take her to the mall to plunder the GAP for all the right college outfits, and had let her tell her that it was one hundred percent the right move to let Chris go - at Duke, there'd be tons of hotter, more sophisticated, more suitable guys than him. Then Stella had headed to New Jersey for Princeton.

The day before her own departure, Chris had showed up at her house. Her mom had put on a subtle yet clear cut sour face but she, Jenna, hadn't given a fuck. „Will you come drive with me for a while?" Chris had asked, and she'd been out of the house in a matter of seconds. As soon as the doors of his truck had closed she'd leaned over to kiss him with all her heart. Her eyes had welled up with tears. „It's alright", he'd said. And he'd taken her to Mayer's fairgrounds where they would sleep together one last time. When they'd laid cuddled up after, she'd tried to apologize for having said that she wanted things he couldn't keep up with. She'd stumbled and stuttered, felt ashamed, loved him so and ended up saying that she hadn't meant it but still thought she should become a lawyer. Chris had said nothing for a moment and then said „It's fine, I guess." And she'd swallowed an abundance of stinging tears.

Before going home, they had sat in the truck for a few more minutes, looking over the field, quiet. And Chris had taken her hand to hold it for a while. It'd been the saddest thing ever.

Another bourbon and coke. That was what she needed. More buzz. She excused herself from Mary's group offering to bring another round of drinks.

She walked over to Wyatt's booth, trying to be invisible. While Wyatt got her order together, she threw a handful of quick glances at Chris.

Saw him playfully punching one of his sons.

Saw him joining a group of friends.

Saw him look around and saw that he was still himself, his face weathered, for sure, the dark brown hair strands that showed under his cap contained an undeniable portion of grey. But other than that he still looked like her Chris. *Stop being so pathetic. Your Chris. Pah.*

Lowering her head and taking a considerable sip of her drink she went back to Mary and her friends.

She was too self conscious to make out what they were talking about. She tried to keep her eyes away from Chris and added things like "interesting!" to the conversation to seem like she was listening.

She was magnetically pulled to the side where Chris stood though and she gave in, turning her head to find that he seemed to look in her direction. She turned her head back at once, freaking out about the possibility that he might have seen her. What if? What if not?

"Their oven cleaner is downright awesome!" Nina exclaimed and Mary looked at Jenna who did not know what to say so she said "I got a cleaning lady."

I should leave, she thought. *Why am I still here? I lost this one.*

But the next moment she shook it off. She had won, she concluded. She had won this long ago. She had won a life that was so much more than having to talk about cleaning or standing around this stupid bonfire year after year. She had evolved, she had grown. Things had worked out according to plan. She was someone. Not to them, here, with minds too narrow to have space for a cosmopolitan, corporate lawyer. But there were people that valued her. Stanford. Darren. Her clients. They understood her. Her expertise, her success, her sophistication. So what was she looking for here? *People grow out of their teenage dreams. You too*, she thought.

"Where are you spending the night?" asked Mary, which brought her back.

"Oh", she collected herself, "I'm not spending the night. I'm going back home. Actually", she checked her phone for effect, "I gotta get going. It's a two hour drive."

Mary lifted her eyebrows at her, looking at her like you would at a child who asks to see an R rated movie. "Didn't you have too much of that bourbon to be driving?"

Waving it off, she said "They weren't that many. I'm fine."

"You as a lawyer should be familiar with a DUI."

She is such a mom.

"I am, Mary, really, I'll be fine. Don't worry."

"Why don't you stay with us tonight?" Mary continued. "What do you say, Kevin?"

"Didn't fix up that guestroom for nothin'", Kevin said turning to them. "You're welcome to stay, Jenna", he said turning back to his conversation with the other guys.

She blushed hard. "Thank you, but, no, that really isn't necessary." *A double wide with fluffy carpets and a baby pink bedspread. No way.* However, she knew that Mary wouldn't let her get away with driving right now. Offering a concession would take weight off. "Alright, maybe it wasn't the best idea to be leaving just now", she said. "I'll just wait a bit until I can drive again. It'll work out fine—"

"Evenin' everyone", someone interrupted her.

His voice hadn't changed one bit. She could have tried to stay in hiding even now, to save herself from chasing after an ex-boyfriend. But she did look at him. And he didn't at her.

"Hi Chris!" Mary said with the others joining in. Kevin waved to Chris' sons who were standing behind him.

"Hey guys", Chris said cheerfully, fist-bumping the men. "How's everything?" Then Chris moved his eyes over to her. He looked at her, she looked back. Her mouth went dry. But she didn't dare to take a sip. It felt as though he waited an eternity to speak. She willed Mary and Beth to be tactful about this.

"Jenna?" he finally said. Asked. "Jenna Briggs?"

"Yeah", she muttered. She wanted to sound conversational, but her voice had suddenly turned croaky. She cleared her throat.

He looked at her. He seemed bewildered, maybe even slightly shocked, which Mary well knew to turn a blind eye to. "Can you believe it!?" she said jubilantly. "She came here tonight. Just out of the blue. From Cincy."

"You don't say", Chris said friendly but reserved — like this was about a car that Mary tried to sell to him and that he wasn't going to go for. "Well hi, Jenna, welcome back. Good to see you." Nothing more. No hug. No quick kiss on the cheek, not even a pat on the shoulder or whatever. No. Thing.

He wore one of those Sherpa jeans jackets, a navy sweater underneath and a black Stetson trucker hat. His build was still pretty youthful, maybe athletic even. She hated that. It would have been much easier had he put on weight or gone bald. His hair had become pretty grey, but she couldn't bring herself to label that as a problem. He looked extremely handsome. Full stop. Asshole.

She felt as out of place as one possibly could and tried an "I'm not back, per se." But he had already turned around. "These are my sons, Sean and Cody", and two teenagers with still insecure handshakes said "Hi" and even "Ma'am" to her. It was the worst.

"Jenna's an old friend from high school."

Old friend.

"Cool", said the younger one. He looked like young Chris which confused her.

"Nice to meet you", said the older one. She said "likewise".

"And you drove here from Cincinnati", continued the older one, which was Cody. She was pretty sure.

"Yes, I live there."

"Wow, that's pretty sweet."

Chris had moved over to Kevin and started talking to the guys.

"I guess. It's a nice place." What to say? For teenagers it was certainly all about shopping malls or sports or concert venues, and she never went to those places. There was nothing about her life that could have made an impression on a teenager.

"Do you go out a lot?" There it was.

"I'm afraid not", she said and tried to chuckle. She felt like an old hag.

While Cody said a few more things about Cincinnati including a favorable mention of the outlets that seemed to be the essence of that city to people here, she tried to think clearly. This was getting completely out of control.

Chris didn't turn around to look at her once.

Could it be that he didn't really remember her anymore? That their relationship had become a faded memory to him, blurred, one of many? Had he lost connection to the impact their relationship had had? Or hadn't it had any impact on him? That surely couldn't be. Or could it?

Cody had finished talking to her, most likely because she hadn't done her part to keep the conversation going. And she thought how wrong she'd been thinking that that Facebook invite had actually meant her, how thin of an argument her broken teenage heart actually was.

"I think I'm ready to drive now", she said to Mary. "It was nice seeing you again."

"No!" Mary protested.

"You can't leave now", Kevin joined in, "I was gonna get us a new round. Stay for one more."

"No, you guys, that's so kind of you, but it's a long drive-"

"We already told you you're welcome to stay in our guest room", Mary insisted.

She saw from the corner of her eye that Chris' sons gestured something to Chris. Then they left.

"Chris was gonna drink one with us. Let's all have a round for old time's sake", Kevin said.

If she said no to that she'd have outed herself as the bitch she most likely was. She swallowed a sigh. "Fine, but only one round." Which made her take in her third bourbon and coke, which postponed her drive to Cincinnati for probably an hour, which meant sixty more minutes of chitter chatter and crumbling hope.

Chris had excused himself quickly after finishing his beer to catch up with others. From time to time, Jenna checked to see whether he'd joined Leslie's group, but so far he hadn't.

She decided to refocus on the conversation happening around her. She heard Beth say "...he is very considerate with her, I really have a good feeling about them", but Jenna suddenly felt like saying *Can you believe I've never actually been to those Cincinnati outlets?* and, thanks to the buzz, she voiced it. The other three stopped talking and looked at her.

"Really?" Nina finally commented, "you live there and have never been?"

"Well, of course I know of them", Jenna said, "I've just never been." She paused for a moment and realized that she had gotten noticeably tipsy; she was dizzy. "Right now I wonder why." Of course she knew why. She wasn't a bargain shopper. Part of her now wished she was.

"Maybe we should all meet up there sometime and make a day of it!" Mary suggested eagerly and everyone cheered, including Jenna. And for a moment she liked to believe that this would actually come to pass.

While she munched another corn dog to get a hold of her buzz so that she would in fact be able to drive back to Cincinnati, she noticed that Mary, Nina and Beth's light-hearted chatter started to give her an unexpected feeling of comfort. The three had just finished bringing her up to speed about how a thermomix elevated the daily business of family life, and had run her through their favorite recipes: rosemary foccacia with feta cheese dip, easy pizza dough and barbecue sauce. And the oddest thing was that she hadn't found this as mundane as she would have thought. She had even quickly had the thought of getting a thermomix for herself, to get a piece of that feeling. Even though she well knew that easy pizza dough was too much of a stretch from Darren's and her meal plan. But still. Her conversations usually centered around work, work and work; sometimes specific cases, how things at the firm were unfolding, sometimes interesting clients. To Darren, she would talk about wines, current affairs, a TED talk she had heard. However, contemplating the question of *What do I talk about with my friends?* only brought her to the simple conclusion: I don't have any friends. Colleagues, a life partner, a Stanford, fellow wine clubbers, a hair dresser, a manicurist, a cosmetologist and a personal trainer, yes. But friends?

She took the last bite of her corn dog. Yes, it frustrated her that Chris Jacobs showed no particular interest in her presence. Not only frustrated her, it was infuriating. But on a deeper level, she was plain sad. Because the truth was that she had never stopped loving him. After a while it probably wasn't so much him anymore, but the memory of him. Of them together. But her feelings for Chris, evidence that she was able to love, had carried her through when she'd doubted that. When she divorced Josh, for example.

Josh was Josh Beringer, a blond surfer-type boy in her literature and history classes. She'd noticed him checking her out every now and then, but he'd only asked her on a date nine months after she'd started at Duke University. She'd agreed to seeing him even though she hadn't been feeling up for romance. She'd been consumed by the thought of never finding love again and had wondered everyday whether she should contact Chris. He hadn't reached out to her, which she knew was what she'd provoked. But she'd hoped and dreamed that he would. Still, when Josh had struck up a chat with her that ended in him asking her if she wanted to have coffee with him sometime, she'd accepted. *Can't stay in this state forever*, she'd thought. At least, Josh'd been endearing. Funny, a born story teller. His career plan of going to med school and then becoming a paediatrician had made perfect sense to Jenna. He'd been so entertaining during their first coffee that the hardened corner of her soul had cracked open with her laughter. And that laughter had been genuine. He came from a family of doctors in Santa Barbara, California, which meant he would be a big hit with her parents, she'd known that right away. His blonde curls made him the all Californian guy, even though he'd said his hair'd become a lot darker and less curly now that he wasn't spending time on his surfboard anymore.

And even though it had felt as though she'd cheated on Chris the first time she'd slept with Josh - though he'd been really and honestly a good guy - she'd enjoyed herself with him. Still, she'd felt the need to draw some lines with Josh when it came to intimacy. She would tell Josh that this or that would make her feel disrespected and used. When really she had absolutely experienced feeling hot and wanted that way. She'd just needed to save something for Chris.

For that reason she'd also avoided taking Josh to her parents as much as possible. She would fake a cold or defer to her parents' busy schedule, or tell Josh that they would much rather come and visit them in Durham. Even two, three, four years later — the thought of being inside Mayer's Creek's city limits with another man still hadn't agreed with her.

On the other hand, visiting his parents in Santa Barbara would turn out to be her annual highlight. California had been a revelation to her. So beautiful, so carefree. By then, she had become aware of her own uptightness. Maybe it had been the influence of the law crowd, maybe her upbringing, or both. She'd felt that she couldn't hop on that relaxed Californian vibe all the way, but she'd managed to let loose a little bit. Yet, when Josh would take her to hang out with his old high school friends, she'd often asked herself what he saw in her. She'd felt so monotonous compared to the girls she would meet there. They were studying design or Spanish literature, and had spent time in Europe. They'd had cool hobbies like surfing, crocheting cute bags or growing their own veggies. She, however, had been exclusively committed to her law degree, intent of being brilliant in her field, and would go to the gym twice a week. That'd been about it. She'd never dared to ask Josh about this, afraid of stirring up something she wouldn't have wanted to stir up. *Opposites attract*, she'd thought, *if he didn't like me he wouldn't stay, right?*

And so, after three years of dating, when Josh had proposed to her surrounded by the salty Californian breeze with the waves gurgling in the background, she'd said yes. They'd gotten married on that same beach, at her suggestion.

She'd worn a chignon at the wedding, her hair sprayed to the twelfth of never so that the pacific breeze wouldn't stand a chance. Her hairdresser had suggested setting her hair in beachy waves, which would have made a lot of sense, but she hadn't been able to bring herself to do that. It just wouldn't have had accorded with the elegance she and her mom had wanted for the wedding. And even though the massive cloud of hair spray had given her a headache that lasted all throughout the ceremony, only very few hair strands had come loose.

She and Josh had moved to California first chance they got, which'd been a year after their wedding. They'd found a cute apartment in south Santa Barbara. Josh had started his residency at the local children's hospital, and she'd managed to obtain a job as associate attorney at a respected Los Angeles law firm. So for a while it had all looked as though it had worked out according to their wishes. But a year in, the daily commute to and from downtown L.A. had been no longer manageable for Jenna. She'd asked Josh what he thought of moving to L.A. He'd chewed on this for a few weeks and then had agreed that it was only fair that he should be commuting as well. It had raised the question of their long term prospects though. *Where will we live in the long run?* he'd asked her but she'd snapped *I'm up to my nose in cases and getting a standing at that firm, let's please talk about that another time*, and had hoped he wouldn't bring it up again any time soon.

Between Josh's shifts at the hospital and her own frequent all-nighters, they'd ended up not seeing a lot of each other that year. And whenever they did manage to have a weekend together, they'd argued. About her all-nighters, which Josh would say weren't healthy, and to which Jenna'd retorted that his night shifts were basically the same thing. He'd say he was saving lives, but to Jenna that had just sounded like he was telling her that his work was more important than hers. How could he!? She'd placed all her bets on this, and she'd been doing well for herself. Hell, she'd had her first informal talk about junior partnership only two years after she had started at that firm, that'd been a tremendous success! Josh should have understood that.

The real beginning of the end, though, was when Josh had brought up their long-term future again. He'd wanted to move out of L.A. to become a father one day. This shouldn't have had come as a surprise to her, yet it had. They'd tried living apart for a while and seeing a marriage counselor. It hadn't been that they hadn't talked about what each of them wanted in life prior to their wedding. It had been that, when they had, Jenna'd been vague, saying things like *Maybe I could see myself having kids one day* and *I definitely wanna live in a nice house sometime in the future*. Meanwhile Josh had most likely heard what he'd wanted to hear.

The truth was that she'd been in no state to commit to anything but to her work. The thought of taking a step back from her career to have one or more children, to risk everything that she had built for herself professionally, had scared the hell out of her. What if she bought the nice house, got the two kids and then realized that none of it made her happy? The path to a successful career in law was clearly laid out and absolutely doable if you followed the rules of the game. *That is all I have* she'd said to him and it took her a few minutes to see how much she must have hurt him by saying that. But that was how it was for her. Her career was everything. Josh was great, but the idea of being his wife without her career had been, well, terrifying. She'd been disappointed at this, too, but not surprised.

The year they'd both turned thirty, she'd suggested they break up, so that Josh could build the life he wanted with someone else. He'd seemed seriously heartbroken when he moved his stuff out of their L.A. apartment. Jenna had suffered from the break up too, of course. A couple years back she had found Josh to be a genuinely good idea, a solid life choice. And now, that plan had gone down the drain. It'd been sad; but it was sad in a different way than the break up from Chris more than ten years earlier. After Chris, it had felt as though her heart had turned numb. Divorcing Josh, on the other hand, had felt like a failure. Like losing a close friend, but not the one you shared your deepest secrets with.

You un-bitch me she had once said to Chris. Of course Chris had cracked up at this because it sounded funny, but for her it had been a vulnerable confession. It had been the concluding comment to an episode she had told him about. Stella Hancock and her at the mall, blowing off and acting above a group of other girls, even insulting them at one point. For no particular reason, Jenna had known that, but she had gone along with it. After having exchanged a few more thoughts on this, Chris had kissed her and said *I know that you're not a bitch, not what it comes down to*. And that had told her that while he had no illusions about the bitch potential in her, his faith in her good heart weighed heavier.

With Josh, she had never shared such conversations.

Still, after he'd left, Jenna'd started feeling like a stranger in California despite her success at the firm. It was as though she had lost her connection to that place, her fiat for being there. She'd eventually decided to contact a headhunter.

Once she'd settled in Cincinnati, she'd quickly realized two things. First, she had unintentionally but undeniably turned into a woman who saw no prospects for her private life. Second, she hadn't been this geographically close to Chris Jacobs in fourteen years. Although the latter realization had made her giddy, she hadn't done anything about it.

So she would immerse herself further in her career. Getting together with Darren two years later hadn't even felt like dating anymore, more like a merger. He was a private equity manager, whom she had met through one of her cases. At that point, she had already given in to Stanford's advances twice. She'd tried to make herself unavailable for as long as possible afterwards, but it only seemed to spur him on. Maybe he thought she was playing hard to get.

In fact, she just wanted to avoid him. Even though she could handle it, even though she could deliver, and even though Stanford was a brilliant lawyer, he repulsed her sexually.

She and Darren quickly moved in together once they'd started dating. Everything was going well. She'd had an interior designer furnish the apartment so elegantly that her mom almost cried. She'd become a senior partner at Gordon & Stanford too. Her next big milestone success would be to become a 'name partner'.

The reasons for these successes laid with Stanford, or rather with Stanford's wife of thirty-five years. She didn't bluntly blackmail him, because something like that was beneath her. But she'd noticed at some point that she spoke in a higher pitch when they saw each other privately, which came in handy for being perceived as a helpless female she'd learn. Combined with a well-orchestrated practice of his liking after his begging, this proved very effective. He felt his secret safe with her, he got what he wanted and rewarded her moral anxiety by treating her more favorably than their other colleagues. It was bribing the jury. End of story. Jenna consoled herself with the fact that she definitely could have made it even without that. Her performance at work was good enough, this little side business merely sped things up. She only played this card when it was really necessary, anyway — just enough for the effect to be sustained.

After a few years of that, her time in California seemed more like a dream. But from time to time, she saw Josh's pictures on Instagram. His most recent photo showed his twin toddlers, and his wife, with a hand resting on her baby belly. *I must be a chapter of his past that he has no explanation for*, she thought. And she thought that she loved California. Not for the fancy hotels that her colleagues went to for a pool vacation. For the rough pacific waves and the salty wind which she hadn't gloried in enough while she had had the chance. She had never told these things to anyone. It was one of the things you don't say out loud. Just like you don't say that you don't like caviar. You just down it and smile.

But the more unreal as her years in California appeared to her, the more real her connection to Chris felt. In a way, it had always been like that. Once, when she sat on the beach while Josh was surfing, she caught herself thinking that Chris would make a great Californian, down to earth and mellow as he was. Or, used to be. Who knew who he was now.

She got torn from her musings by a voice right next to her.

"Can I get you a drink?"

She looked up to see Chris standing there. But it still took her a moment to remind herself of where she was. Bonfire Night in Mayer's Creek. 2024. She was holding a nibbled off corn dog stick in her hand.

"Hi", she said, abruptly realizing that Chris had come alone, no sons, no Leslie. "Hi" he said, smiling a bit. He looked her up and down for a moment. "I like your shirt." He reached out, gently pulling the collar of her puffer coat to aside so he could get a better view at her shirt. His shirt.

Jenna held her breath. He'd noticed the shirt. Not only that, he'd reached out and touched her.

"Thank you", she pressed out, swallowing hard. She looked away because looking at him seemed like dangerous territory. "Alright. A drink. Why not."

Chris didn't speak again until after they'd said cheers and taken a sip. "Jenna Briggs", he said then, "wasn't sure if I'd ever see you again."

Shit. "Me neither", she said, "funny, huh?"

"That so? Then why did you come tonight?"

Her heart was racing. "Oh, I, uhm", she stumbled, issuing a short nervous laugh, "I don't know, I... I suddenly felt like it."

Chris nodded thoughtfully. Jenna wished he would let her off the hook. Go easy on her.

"What I mean is, I get that I've been a no-show for a while", she tried and shrugged helplessly. That made him burst out laughing which was classic Chris. He'd always cracked up when she'd been struggling.

"What!?" Her sharp tone made Chris stop laughing. "You were—" he stopped. "You know what, never mind. How've you been?"

Saved by the bell. At least this was a question she could answer. "Good", she said, "Thanks. And you?"

"Meh, sometimes better, sometimes worse. The last few years've been pretty good, though." Chris took another sip of his beer without looking away. Jenna wondered if she was allowed to ask after the ‚sometimes worse' part, but he continued to speak. "But what about you, you've been just good? The whole twenty years and all?"

"Pretty much. Of course I've had my fair share of bad days, but everybody has those, right? But on the whole...," she nodded eagerly. He went on to ask her whether she had become a lawyer after all, and she in turn inquired if the tittle-tattle she'd once heard, which had been that he sold cars, was true.

He chuckled. "Yeah I used to do that, but I breed horses full-time now. Much more exciting. Though probably not as exciting as being a lawyer."

That stung her. "No", she intervened quickly, "it's very exciting." Suddenly she was able to look directly into his eyes. Of course Chris still loved horses. And she still cherished the memory of visiting them, together. She felt a lump in her throat. What he'd just said touched her. "It's very exciting", she repeated determinedly. "Good for you." She smiled, anchoring herself in his brown eyes for the first time in so many years. He answered her smile, and for a moment everything seemed possible. Then Chris chuckled and tore himself out of that moment. He rubbed over his face quickly and said "Oh gosh." But he returned to looking at her, uttering a boyish giggle, and she laughed a bit as well. Then he bashfully stretched his arms and suggested going back over to Mary and Kevin and the rest.

And so they did and Mary and her friends were happy to find that Jenna was still there. The ensuing conversation wasn't about anything special, just more small-talk and everyday matters. Although she and Chris were standing next to each other, which could have very well lead to associations or flashbacks of a certain kind, no one brought up the past at all. Maybe it was all too long ago. Maybe it wasn't in force anymore.

For Jenna however, standing next to Chris in a group of old friends at Bonfire Night, was exhilarating. She couldn't help but remembering the olden days when she would hold Chris' hand on this occasion, and she couldn't help but getting caught up in the image of them being a couple again.

Another hour later the crowd had thinned considerably. After talking with her husband, Mary turned to Jenna and said: "Honey, we're going to call it a night. Are you coming with us?"

"Oh, that's such a kind offer, but as I've said, it's best for me to just drive home."

Mary frowned at her. "Jenna, come on. It's nearly midnight and you've been drinking all evening. You're not going to get in your car to drive two hours."

Chris, who had been listening to Mary and Jenna, turned to the latter and said decisively: "Yeah you shouldn't risk it. Just stay with Mary."

Jenna tightened her body so that she wouldn't melt on the spot. Was Chris campaigning for her to spend the night in Mayer's Creek? Was he worried for her well-being on a possible drive to Cincinnati? Was he taking care of her?

If Jenna was staying, though, she didn't wanna stay at Mary's.

"But I didn't bring any toiletries", was the best she could come up with.

"Not to worry, we have spare toothbrushes." Mary said, not taking the hint.

Jenna tried to think quickly, but her mind was blank. She sighed. "Okay, fine", she finally said, "I'll stay over. Thank you Mary." Her agreement made both Mary and Chris smile. "That's the right decision for sure", Chris said, "it's way too late for a drunk Jenna to drive all that way." He rubbed his hands together. "Alright then, you guys have a good night." He hugged first Mary and then Kevin, the latter in a bear hug, mightily patting his back a few times.

"Alright, let's go", Mary finally said, interrupting their hug. That was Jenna's cue to leave. Just when she unavailingly racked her brain again for some way to spend a few more minutes with Chris, he grabbed her by the arm and said "stay", which made her freeze in place. Helplessly, she looked towards Mary's retreating back. Kevin had wrapped his arm around her and they're weren't waiting or looking back for her.

Jenna looked at Chris. Although she felt scared now that she was alone with Chris, she couldn't wait for it to happen.

"Will you finally say something about the shirt?" he said.

Although they both knew that it was really too late to drink more, they walked over to Wyatt's. Chris had let the matter with the shirt drop after she'd said: "It could have been yours, I guess." This was the most she could share in that moment. For some reason she was afraid of giving herself away. He gave her a look that made clear he didn't buy it. But this was who she was.

Chris waved his empty cup to get her attention. "You sure you're up for one more?"

For the first time tonight, the question of a drink wasn't a matter of 'should I' or 'shouldn't I'. "Yeah."

"Will you make us two highballs, Wyatt?" Chris said and placed their cups on the counter.

"Wait a minute!" Wyatt burst out, pointing at her. "Now I know who you are. You two used to be lovebirds way back!" She blushed and said "Yeah, way back."

"I've been racking my brain all night, trying to figure out how I knew you", Wyatt continued. As he got the bottle of bourbon out, Chris gave her a quick smile. Then he turned to Wyatt. "Make it a proper one Wyatt, this one's for old times' sake."

"You got it," Wyatt said and poured the bourbon generously.

She waited until Chris was ready, then took a sip at the same time as him. Chris' eyes flew open. "Fuck", he said, "that's more bourbon than coke!"

"Yeah, no shit", Jenna confirmed. She noticed that she never talked like that anymore but enjoyed it now. "I'm not sure I'm gonna survive this fuckin' highball", she added, savouring the 'fuckin'', and Chris laughed as though she'd said something funny.

"Do you wanna get closer to the band?" Chris asked. "Appreciate their last few songs before they're done for tonight?" Jenna nodded. And just like that, Chris took her hand. Even squeezed it quickly. "Alright then, come." Jenna felt as though instead of walking with him, she was rather stumbling along. He had completely taken her by surprise. A wonderful surprise, no doubt, but in a way too overpowering for her to go along with. Her hand felt tense and insecure inside his.

She wished she would be able to shake that off. Maybe the combination of music and bourbon could do the trick.

When Chris had found a spot that seemed fitting to him, he let go of her hand and pointed to the ground. "Wanna sit down here?" She must have shot him a confused look, because he continued to say: "Look, I'm sorry, but there aren't any leather couches or whatever you're used to around here. It's no big deal." And he sat himself down. *Get a grip*, she thought and said as pertly as possible: "I sit on the ground all the time", taking her seat next to him. Once again, Chris only laughed. "Sure", he said, "sure you do!" But instead of trying to cover up how stupid she felt, she just joined his laughter. It sounded liberating, and she wanted to feel some piece of that.

"So, what made you come here tonight?" Chris asked her yet again.

"I got an invitation on Facebook", she said, taking a sip of her drink.

"Really?"

"Really."

"Okay, then what made you accept it?" Ugh. He didn't want to let her off the hook.

"I... I suddenly felt like doing something... crazy. I guess." *'Let's do something crazy' is not. My. Vocabulary.*

Chris burst out laughing. "Something crazy?" He gave her a disbelieving look.

"What!?" she managed to say.

"You are one crazy lawyer."

"What does that even mean?" The same laughter that had sounded liberating to her a minute ago now started to irritate her. Why didn't he take her more seriously? "Why do you keep asking these things!?"

"You're wearing my shirt."

"Is that a reason to make fun of me?"

"It's a reason to ask questions."

"Why don't I give you the 3rd degree like that? I bet there's lots I could ask you about."

"No there isn't", Chris said quickly. "There's nothing unusual about me, or me being here. I'm doing what I always do this time a year. Getting drunk at Bonfire Night. Me, I've been doing this for twenty-five years. But you? You haven't."

This made her blush and once again, Jenna had to compose herself. "Fine. So I was in the mood for..." *Don't say it.* "Nostalgia."

"Nostalgia," he repeated. He thought for a moment, nodding slightly. "Ok then, let's give you what you came for." He got up and held his hand out to her. "Wanna dance?" That sent a shiver down her spine. While trying to remember the last time she'd danced, she let him pull her up. „Give me that." He took her half-emptied cup and put it on the ground with his. "We'll get those later." They walked closer to the stage where only a handful of people were dancing. Jenna concluded that it had been ten, twelve years since her last dance. It had likely taken place at some wedding that she had attended with Josh. She had no idea what to do once Chris would start dancing with her, and that freaked her out.

The band had just started playing 'I Am A Man Of Constant Sorrow' for about the third time tonight, but the woman who played the banjo didn't seem to get tired of it. She appeared to have a party up there regardless of the late hour. In the spirit of the song's lively beat, Chris took Jenna's hand, turned her jauntily to him, put his other hand on her waist and started to sway her around. He left her no chance to evaluate the situation first; her nervousness, her longing, her intoxication, her ignorant feet. He lead her, turning her this way and that, pulling her in and twirling her back out. *Is that a two step?* she wondered, but even if it were she wouldn't have known what to do. Yet, although her feet had no clue of the protocol, she made it work by following Chris' confidence.

And so she placed her hand on his shoulder and let it happen. She had never danced with him like that before, only slow dances to pop music. The way he smiled at her whenever their eyes met radiated genuine happiness, and affection rose in her. Affection that would surely bite her in the ass at some point, but for now she wanted to give in and she smiled back warmly.

Then the song was over and the band announced their final number for the night. "It's Chris Stapleton's 'Broken Halos', so grab your sweetheart for a last dance", the singer said. And Chris pulled Jenna closer to him and softly swayed back and forth with her. And she wanted to drown in his eyes, erase the last twenty years and do it all over together with him. Get married, move into a house, drive around in his truck, be the two of them against the rest of the world. She laid her head on his shoulder, he wrapped his arms around her and brought his face closer to hers so that she could feel his breath on the bridge of her nose.

"Come", he whispered after a while. He took her hand while the song continued to play and lead her away from the fire. While they walked towards the few remaining parked cars, she noticed that his hand felt calloused, probably from rough labor. Her well-manicured fingers intertwined with his, and any tension from before disappeared.

Chris took her behind what was presumably his truck. He leaned her against the passenger door, and before she knew what was happening, locked lips with her. Jenna's heart raced. Raced hard. Even though the dancing had made them get closer, Chris' kiss somehow came unexpected. She kissed back. Not as decidedly as he kissed her, with his arms wrapped around her waist, pulling her close. But she answered. And finally surrendered. It was a kiss like none Jenna had had in recent years. A real one. One where you have no way of not kissing.

Kissing Chris was a lot like she remembered, but it was also new. No wonder, after all these years. The tickly, soft stubble on his face was new, he'd never had that as a teenager. He kissed her warmly and passionately, like he always had, but his moves were more polished, more gentleman-like now. Jenna enjoyed every bit of it. And she hoped that he would be just as much into kissing her. She freaked out about the possibility that she could have gotten too uptight for things like these over the years when he whispered: "I seriously thought I'd never see you again."

"Me too", she simply whispered back.

"If you had told me thirty minutes ago that this would happen, I wouldn't have believed you." he said while his hands were finding her butt under the puffer coat. She had a hard time pulling herself together and focusing on the conversation, hot as it felt. "Tell me about it", she said, laughed a bit and reached up to his face to kiss him again.

But all of a sudden he pulled back, took her face in his hands and looked her straight in the eyes. "Don't play games, Jenna", he whispered. Why would he say that?

She held on to his eyes. She felt a multitude of things.

"You were right about the shirt", she whispered back, anxious.

A moment.

"Are you ready to give it back to me?"

She held her breath. She hoped he wouldn't see the uncertainty in her eyes. It wasn't that she didn't want to be with him. It was all she wanted. But things had become so messed up lately.

"I don't mean here, obviously. We're not sixteen anymore." He waited, but Jenna couldn't think of how to reply. She bit her lip to keep her composure and nodded.

"I was thinking of some place free from prying eyes," Chris said, winking. Despite the cocky wink, she detected some scepticism in his voice. No wonder. She must have seemed uninterested.

She managed to get a hold of herself for long enough to give him a flirty "What a gentleman!"

Chris smiled. "I can be, if you want. But I would have thought you'd be sick of gentlemen by now."

"What?"

"I was figuring some, uh, rugged working man might be more interesting for you. A breath of fresh air, you know." Her stomach tickled like crazy when he clicked the truck open. She knew that her entire condition was fragile, but she still put on a catty look and said: "Rugged... should I be scared?"

"Only a little bit", he said when he held the truck door open for her. Climbing in, Jenna felt that long lost combination of eroticism and trust rising inside of her. She welcomed the feeling. She'd missed it.

On the drive they didn't say much.

The question *Is he gonna take me to his family's home?* suddenly popped up in her head and spooked her. He wouldn't do that, right? Should she ask him about Leslie?

She considered it for a moment, but something kept her from posing that question. She admitted to herself that it didn't matter to her, even if that attitude was morally questionable. But it wasn't like she had lived morally impeccably for the past few years anyway. On the other hand, it was absolutely essential for her to treat the thing with Chris differently than the thing with Darren and Stanford. She tensed up thinking those names and shook her head a bit to get rid of them.

"Everything alright?" Chris asked.

"Yeah, sure", she said quickly.

She wanted to be able to believe she was the only one. That was it. She didn't wanna be second runner up after his tanned bitch wife. So she kept quiet and just let him take her to his place.

Which was, apparently, at a ranch. It was a house in the style of a log cabin lit with two outside lights. Chris killed the engine and jumped out of the truck to open the door for her.

Earlier, Chris had told her that he bred horses. It made sense that he'd live on a ranch, but Jenna hadn't expected one that looked so cozy and homey. It made her hesitate. It wasn't just Leslie. He had a family. A wife was handleable, but children were something else entirely.

"Aren't your sons home?" she asked shyly.

"No", he said. "They're probably out in some field, drinking. I mean, Cody is." He winked at her. "Like us. Then." She would have loved to give in to that memory but she was too anxious. "Sean's at his mom's", Chris added.

Jenna kept her cool but felt her heart skip a beat. *His mom's.* That didn't sound like happily ever after.

She took a deep breath, climbed out of the truck, and the two of them started walking up to the front door.

Unlike the pretty outside of the house, the interior resembled a construction zone.

"Sorry about the state of the place", Chris said, closing the front door behind her. "I'm doing most of the building and handiwork myself, and I only have so much time left for it at the end of the day. But the basic rooms are done." He helped her out of her puffer coat and hung it on a hook next to the door. Then he took off his own jacket while Jenna took a look around. "That is so impressive. That you do all this by yourself."

Chris seemed proud at that, but downplayed it. "Oh, not really, I just wanna save money."

In the still empty space adjoining the kitchen area, attached to two wooden beams, she discovered a hammock. She couldn't help but smile. Patios in Santa Barbara had had hammocks.

"You have a hammock." She said wistfully.

"Yeah, I like to unwind in there." He seemed to notice the change in her, because he looked at her somewhat curiously. "Do you like hammocks?"

She looked up, right at him. „Yeah", she said decidedly, ignoring the fact that she made up her mind about them only now. She associated them with California, but no more than palm trees or Pinkberry. But she wanted to believe that this meant something. That they were in California as well as in Chris' house.

"Have you ever tried... stuff... in a hammock?" he asked her, flirting.

Blushing, she said "No!" and started laughing. "I would think it's way too shaky in there for... that."

"Damn right it is," he laughed, too. "Gotta be an acrobat to get down to business in there."

They looked at each other until their laugher faded. "Do you want some water?" Chris asked, and Jenna affirmed, mainly because it meant that there would be a plan for the next few minutes.

He went over to the fridge and she followed him, stopping at the kitchen island. Chris grabbed two bottles of water, and handed one of them to her. They stood opposite each other, the island between them. They each opened their bottle and drank some.

Jenna had no clue what to do after these sips of water. She knew what was in the air, wanted it herself, but how to get from this to that was beyond her. With Darren, she'd last had sex over a year ago. With Stanford, she followed a tried and tested routine. In any case, her experiences with Darren or Stanford were not to be consulted here. The last thing she wanted was to be that Jenna with Chris.

She got annoyed with herself. Why had she been able to drive a hundred and thirty miles to see him, but was incapable of bridging these last two feet, of circumnavigating that damn island!? When she was sure, too, that he waited for her to make a move.

A few moments went by. *Fuck it.*

She cleared her throat and dared to say: "So, you want me to give you back the shirt?"

He shrugged, withstanding her gaze. "I really only want you to take it off." She felt as though she was about to lose it, but Chris came to her, took her water bottle and put it down. "Let me see..." He started unbuttoning the shirt and gave her a look that she knew all too well. And she loved him for that look, loved that it hadn't gone away in twenty years. *I want you*, that look said. *I'll protect you.* She had come for exactly this look, and now that she had it, she only thought *I can't do it. I shouldn't do it.* She simply didn't trust herself anymore. Giving Stanford blowjobs was disgusting, but at least she didn't need to be herself. But here, with Chris, Jenna didn't want to just adopt some persona and zone out. She couldn't, and wouldn't, do that to him.

Tears rose in her eyes, it was pathetic, she was pathetic, but she couldn't prevent it.

Of course Chris noticed and stopped what he was doing. He seemed genuinely worried. "Jenna! Are you alright?"

She went for a somewhat brave smile. "Yeah."

Chris frowned. "Are you sure?" He sighed, then continued: "Don't take this the wrong way, but this isn't the first time tonight that you seem... off. Is something going on?"

A moment. When she didn't reply, he added: "I thought you wanted this."

She clung to that. "Yes", she said under her breath. "I do. Just... go on."

"Are you sure?"

Jenna plastered the fakiest grin on her face. "It's just the combination of bourbon and nostalgia. Sorry. I'm good to go now."

"Yeah, maybe", he said. For a long moment, he just looked at her. Then he cleared his throat and looked down. "Don't get me wrong, because for most of the night I've barely been able to think of anything except sleeping with you. But you seem super uncertain right now." His eyes met hers again. "I guess I'm a gentleman after all." He chuckled. Effortlessly. He wasn't messed up like her, he was just there, being himself. She envied him for that.

"Chris, please", she nearly begged. Not knowing what else to say, she helplessly shook her head. Getting out of that shirt seemed to be the last resort, so she did and held it out to him. She shivered reflexively when her curls pleasantly tickled her arms, giving her goosebumps. And it was this sensation that lead her to reconnecting with her old, long ago self. She had stood in front of Chris like this many times. In a bra and pants, her hair softly covering her shoulders and breasts. Maybe she could take it from there. Hopefully. "Here", she said.

He looked at her, smiling gently. "You're as beautiful as always, did you know that?"

It was now or literally never. He wouldn't take the shirt, so Jenna let it drop on the kitchen floor. She moved closer to him and reached for his face. "Where is the bed?" she whispered. He started guiding her backwards while they kissed. He opened the door to his bedroom with one hand before putting it on her waist again.

She felt that he wanted to take his sweet time with her, but she had to minimize the risk of her backing out. Therefore, it needed to happen instantly. She sped through undressing herself and him, too much in a rush to savor and enjoy him. When he pinned her down with his strong, naked body, it was as though she had made it to the end. She let out a breath of relief.

And then she clung to his eyes. *Just give yourself over to him, he'll take care of you.* She didn't know anymore what was real and what was her phantasy of him. She didn't care. She made love to him as well as to all those memories of them. And desperately hoped that feeling him would create clarity. And yes, after a while something melted within her. She felt soft. And she was close to losing all control, so close that she could barely keep in the *I love you.*

When she opened her eyes the next morning she needed a moment to remember where she was. As soon as she figured it out a wave of warmth rolled through her. She sleepily turned her head to Chris, only to find that the bed was void of him.

Where was he?

More importantly: why wasn't he here?

Why had he gotten up already?

She sniffed a bit to make out if there was a whiff of coffee in the air; if there was, he'd simply gotten up to make her breakfast. But she couldn't detect any.

It wasn't good news when a man runs from the bed before the woman he just slept with wakes up. Her throat tightened. Disappointment rose in her, but, more than that, she quickly felt dumb and utterly embarrassed. How could she be so stupid as to assume that the whole thing had been more to him than just a fuck? She had been so consumed by her own sorry-ass emotions regarding the reunion with Chris that she'd lacked any capacity to perceive what this was to him: scoring with his ex, a ridiculously sad woman with a full blown midlife crisis. And he had seen her almost fall apart last night, dear god!

She needed to get the hell out of there. She jumped out of bed, collected her clothes from the floor and put them on. What a jerk. What a total asshole! She needed no crap from a roughneck like him, when she was a dignified, classy lawyer.

On the way out, though, she saw the lumberjack shirt. It was still laying on the kitchen floor where she had dropped it the night before. She stopped short, swallowing hard. *How could he do this to me?* Feeling defeated, she picked up that shirt, put on her coat and exited the house.

Outside, she heard an engine running in the distance. Chris was nowhere to be seen, but she wasn't really looking for him, either. He didn't deserve to have her searching for him. She started walking down the driveway and took out her phone in order to call a cab. She got distracted by Darren's fifteen missed calls and his twelve messages, ranging from "Call me now!" to "Where the hell are you!?" and even one "I am worried!" Two messages were from Stanford, who told her to check her emails regarding the Jarbers Inc. case and get back to him asap. She tapped the 'call' button automatically. Stanford picked up only a second later.

"This is unlike you", Stanford said. He meant the fact that she hadn't called within an hour of him sending the emails.

"I was out of town", she said half-heartedly. Meanwhile, the engine sound got louder.

"Sounds good. We should make a day of it the next time you get out of town."

She felt her voice pitch up when she said "That would be lovely", but it got drowned out by the sound of the engine. Whatever vehicle that was had to be right behind her.

"I'm sorry, I'm kinda in the middle of something." She started to walk faster down the driveway. She wanted to escape and wasn't up to finding out where that noise was coming from.

"What the hell are you doing!?" Stanford shouted.

Finally. The engine turned off. "Jenna! Hey, Jenna, wait!"

Chris.

She did turn around at that and saw Chris climb down a parked compact tractor, all the while inventing some story about visiting her hometown in rural Kentucky for Stanford. Chris was jogging towards her. In a quick movement, she stuffed the plaid shirt down the back of her pants. She told Standford „I'll call you from the car." and hung up. Reluctantly, she looked at Chris.

"Are you leaving?" he asked.

"Yes. I have to get back to Cincinnati", she said. "That was my boss on the phone."

Chris nodded. Looked at her somewhat puzzled. "That's too bad."

Are you kidding me? she thought, but simply said: "I have a lot of work to do. Would've done it last night, but..." It was difficult to keep eye-contact with him, but at this point, that was a matter of pride. She braced herself for an argument, but all that happened was that the warmth left Chris' eyes. „Yeah", he said again, "that's too bad." He lifted a shoulder in a shrug and pursed his lips. "You should get going then. Don't wanna keep your boss waiting." He turned away, walked back to his tractor and climbed on the seat. He didn't start the engine though. Instead, he fixed her, his eyes flashing angrily. She stared back, unable to move. Then he did start the engine. Turning the wheel, he gave her a scoffing grin.

That was enough. She should have turned around right this second, gotten to her car, and focused on Jarbers Inc. But instead, she walked towards Chris.

"What the hell is going on with you!?" She had to scream, loud as the engine was.

"What's wrong with me!?" Chris was yelling back, his voice going raspy. "You're the one who can't get away fast enough. Sure brings back some vivid memories!" He put the tractor in reverse gear and started slowly driving backwards. Away from her.

"Excuse me!?!" she shouted. What the fuck was he thinking, abandoning her in his bed and now turning it into her fault!

He must have not been able to hear her over the noise because he didn't react. *Turn around! Go home!* she told herself. But instead she started following the retreating tractor. "Hey!" No reaction. Since he was rolling pretty slowly, she simply jumped on the step and grabbed his leg in order to not fall off.

"What the fuck!" Chris put on the breaks.

"Shut off the damn thing!" she demanded.

He held her stare for a moment, then gave in and switched off the tractor.

Jenna let go of his leg and held on to the steering wheel instead. "I wanna know what the hell you were saying before. Brings back memories!?"

He sighed. "Jenna", he said rubbing his eyes. "I don't need your shit."

But she insisted. "What was that supposed to mean!?"

Chris looked up at her, utterly blank-faced. "What did I mean? I meant you haven't changed a bit. A fancy college wants you — you jump the gun and leave. A fancy boss wants you — you jump the gun. And leave. I see a fuckin' pattern!"

She felt her cheeks heat up. "Shut up about my boss! You haven't got the slightest idea what it means to work for an AV rated law firm!"

"You're damn fuckin' right I don't, and I don't want to! So please", he resolutely stretched his arm out pointing down the driveway, "go ahead, leave! Jump the gun, suck up to your boss, to your clients, whatever blows your dress up! Just don't expect me to cheer you on or even approve of it, because I don't! I did that once and I regretted it for years!"

Even though Jenna's mouth had fallen open, she was quick to collect herself. "You left me to wake up alone! Tell me, Chris, who does that!?"

A moment.

Then he shook his head, letting out a disbelieving laugh. "The horse rancher who needs to feed his animals does that. Every fuckin' morning."

Just don't lose face.

"Sorry for assuming you'd apply common sense", he added, looking exhausted. "I was hoping you'd sleep till after I was done and we could have coffee together."

I would... have loved that.

"But obviously, your boss is waiting for you. I mean... what can ya do, huh?"

She closed her eyes for a second as though to reset herself. The laughing, the dancing, the drinking and kissing and lovemaking whirled through her mind. As well as an echo of Chris' *I regretted it for years.*

"You should have left a note, Chris", she finally said. "But my boss can wait for a bit." She had managed to calm herself a little bit. And noticed that she felt lonely. "I think coffee would be good."

Chris sighed. "Alright. Sure. But no more shit, Jenna." She nodded barely noticeably. Chris patted his tractor. "Let me just park this thing. I'll be right back to make us that coffee."

Jenna let go of the steering wheel and jumped down. As Chris drove off, she felt as though she'd been summoned to court. Her heart pounded nervously, and she habitually started to collect arguments. *No more shit* he'd said.

She sat on a bar stool at the island, drumming her fingers on the counter. Was there any way for her to argue this case as the plaintiff? Playing the *'you ran out on waking up together'*-card seemed like a weak strategy. But no other option came to her mind. *He's going to want to make you the defendant. Watch out for that.*

She heard his footsteps approach the door. Then he entered, took off his jacket, washed his hands in the sink and took a can with ground coffee from one of the wall cabinets. He still had a good, old coffee machine. Jenna wondered why. She realized that she found it a little weird. She'd have expected at least a Keurig.

Like he knew what she was thinking, he said: "I only have filtered coffee. Sorry if you were expecting fancier. Is that alright?"

"Yeah", Jenna said, "of course." She wondered if being so agreeable would make her the defendant. Most likely. *Damn it.* But she also wanted him to make peace with her.

He closed the water tank and switched on the machine. Then he turned around, leaned against the counter behind him and crossed his arms. He looked at her expectantly. "So. What was going on before?"

"I had a lot of things going on all at once. I was stressed, what with my boss on the phone yelling, not knowing how to get to my car", she took a deep breath. "And I thought you'd just abandoned me—"

"You know what, Jenna, I don't need a rerun of the show out there!" He interrupted her harshly, taking a step towards the island. "Let me get something straight: If I'd wanted a quick fuck I would have gotten one from you, believe me! You weren't exactly steadfast last night. I wouldn't even have had to bring you here for that! I mean", he sounded aghast, "you show up here after twenty. Fucking. Years! Without so much as a text first. How hard is it in times of ICT to get a hold of someone, huh!? Instead you appear out of the blue, playing friends with Mary, whom you haven't given a shit about in forever. And wearing that old shirt of mine as some costume for all I know, probably in order to push my buttons! Which you succeeded at, congratulations, well... sue me! It's you for crying out loud. And, don't get me wrong", he gestured at Jenna, "you're as hot as ever! But—" He paused and took a breath while lifting his hat and smoothing his hair back, "you don't say a fucking word." His voice had suddenly calmed down. It sounded tired now. "Something real, I mean. Not your manipulative shit."

A moment.

"I danced to your damn whistle when we broke up. I won't do that again."

Dumbfounded, Jenna barely dared to breathe. Chris' last words had cut her to the heart. She looked at him hesitantly, saw how upset he was. But her mind spun, and she couldn't get a hold of it.

Suddenly, she heard herself say, "I'm having sex with my boss." She had no idea why, out of all the things she could have said right then, she picked those words. Chris seemed just as surprised.

"What?"

She realized that she'd have to explain herself now. Shit. But there was nothing for it. "My boss, the guy I was talking on the phone with, I'm" she paused to chose her words, "making myself available to him." She let that linger for a moment, feeling embarrassed. Then she scoffed. "I have no idea why I told you that. Forget it."

"I won't." he said stubbornly. The coffee machine hissed. Chris looked up, seemingly having forgotten the coffee. Then he turned to get mugs and milk.

She scrutinized him. Even though it felt as though millions of miles had come between them since last night, he was still familiar to her. His movements had always reminded her of dancing. When he changed his weight from one foot to the other to close the fridge, he would cock his hip a bit. When he turned around to hand her a coffee mug, he did it on one foot, like a pirouette. Twenty years hadn't changed this. A wave of affection rushed through her, and she knew what she should say to him.

Compromise. "I do it for my career."

"What?"

She stared into her coffee, couldn't bring herself to look into his eyes for this. "Sex with my boss. I do that because it's good for my career."

She heard him click his tongue. "If you say so."

She looked up to him, tried to say "It's not that simple." But then she thought, what if it was, what if Chris felt that way because he'd changed his own life. Chris had always appeared so effortless to her in everything he did, but who said that it hadn't been scary and difficult for him to start this ranch?

She felt like running on empty. She drank some coffee.

Leaning against the counter again, Chris eyed her for a moment. Then: "So, shagging up with your boss. Anyone else I should know about?"

She blushed. "Yeah, I'm with a guy, his name's Darren."

Chris nodded. "And, let me guess. Darren doesn't know about your boss."

"Of course not!"

The room fell silent again. Jenna tried to come up with something to say. Before she could, Chris cleared his throat and said quietly: "Last night, when I first saw you, I didn't know how to handle you being there." He looked down, rubbing his fingers, obviously trying to decide something. She was anxious for what else he might say.

"Why didn't you write?"

Couldn't he just cut her some slack? "Chris, I drove here on a whim, I didn't plan—"

"I don't mean now." He looked at her. "Back in the day, after you moved to Durham."

Her palms started sweating. *You know why*, she thought. B*ecause of my mom, because of the Stella Hancocks of this world. Because I needed you to stay* *out of my life or I wouldn't have been able to hold it together.*

"I heard that you started dating Leslie Smitts. I thought a letter would have been out of place", she said, trying hard to sound straightforward.

"Leslie and I didn't start dating until a year after you left", Chris told her, "a year is plenty of time for one damn email."

What do you want from me? she thought helplessly, feeling ashamed. All she'd done had been trying to make the right decision. Couldn't that be factored in? "You didn't write either", she said.

"I did."

Silence.

"What!? When!?" She felt that something was on the verge of caving in. She just didn't know what that something was.

"During your first few months at college. I sent you four emails. Four! Asking whether you'd had a good start and how everything was going. Told you I missed you, too, sore loser that I was."

A lump formed in her throat. "I never gave you my email address", she forced out.

Chris scoffed. "I know you didn't. I had to ask around for it. In the end, Mary got it for me from your mom. She'd put down your cell number, too." Jenna swallowed. "I never even used that", Chris added, "since you didn't answer a single email."

"But—" she interrupted herself. Could this be? "Chris, please, I never got those emails." Although she kept her manner composed, her voice did sound pretty pleading. "And I always check my spam folder."

Words got stuck in Jenna's throat. *What if I had...* No. She couldn't go down that road. All she knew was that she could kill her mother.

"I'm glad to hear that" he said, not without melancholy, and added "Well, in a way... So yeah, I started dating Leslie. I mean, not as a direct reaction to you not writing. Just as a means to move on."

She had to pull herself together hard. She couldn't break down in front of him twice after seeing him for the first time after so many years. She prayed that her voice wouldn't break. "And... were or are you married to her?"

"No."

A relieved laugh burst out of her, for all that she still thought that made no sense. After all, he still had his sons. They couldn't have come from no one.

He looked at her puzzled.

"I'm sorry, it's just... I met Leslie at the bonfire last night, and since my last info was that you dated her, I imagined you were still together. Which is totally stupid, I see that now. But I had a couple of moments where I imagined she... spied on us—"

He laughed a bit, shaking his head. "Oh my god. Women."

"Tell me about it", she said, and an image of Mary's friends winking at her flashed through her mind. " T h e reason I have my boys is that I was married to Tammy, for a bit. Czerkowski, if you remember her."

She searched her brain. "Oh... Tammy! Wasn't she a bit younger than us?"

"Yeah, she was a sophomore when we graduated. I wasn't careful with her and got her pregnant about six months after we started going out." He shrugged. "We had a couple of rough years, I mean, I was twenty four, she was twenty two when Cody was born, we barely knew each other. We were young, we did what we could, but four years ago we called it quits." He stopped for a moment. "But my boys are the best. They're great kids, I'm really glad and thankful to have them. They live with me half the time. Their rooms are on the upper floor." Chris pointed up. "Sean is at Tammy's this weekend, but Cody's plan was to decide spontaneously where he'd spend the night. I texted him after you'd fallen asleep. New experience, giving my sixteen year-old the heads up that I had someone over."

"I'm sorry for causing you trouble." Jenna said.

Chris took a deep breath, gave her a courteous grin and a wink and said "Well, Madam, that wasn't the trouble."

How could she not be smitten with him? She smiled. "Your younger son reminds me of you." she said softly.

Chris chuckled. "Yeah, Sean definitely takes after me." He looked at her. "You ever thought about having kids?"

She blushed. "No."

They fell silent again. Chris continued to lean on the counter, looking at Jenna. She revelled in the sight of him. He looked beautiful in that older, masculine way. He was still this gentle, understanding man; he was caring, but also decisive. And honest. Even better, he was only two steps away from her. First love, last love, they say. And they were right.

She got up and went over to him. Came up on her toes, took his face in her hands and kissed him. He wrapped his arms around her. She thought, *I never want to kiss anybody else like that ever again.*

"I have to get going", she finally said.

"I'll take you to your car", he whispered.

The moment she took place in the passenger seat of his truck, she felt the bundled up lumberjack shirt in her back that was still stuffed down her jeans. She tried to ignore it as much as possible. She would neatly hang it into the back of her closet again and steal a peek at it once in a while, daydreaming about returning it to its rightful owner.

The ranch was outside of town, secluded, with no other buildings around. When they'd arrived here last night, it had been dark and she wasn't able to look at their surroundings. But in the daylight, it was beautiful. Horses were grazing on green meadows peppered with yellow and blue flowers. Chris drove past them down a long gravel road, that took them to the street that lead into Mayer's Creek.

The town had changed a lot. Most of the stores and restaurants were new. Only the two gas stations and the big grocery store were where they had always been. Although the grocery store belonged to a different chain now.

She thought of Mary, how nice she had been to her last night. Maybe she'd reach out to her and thank her for letting her join her and her group for the evening. Jenna had genuinely enjoyed it. She would write that. And mean it, for once. She wrote so many things, formulated so many paragraphs, and it all never made a difference to her. But she was looking forward to writing Mary, because that would matter.

A wet pile of ashes where the fire had been was the only trace of last night. The few vendors must have already taken down their booths earlier in the morning. Chris parked right behind Jenna's Mercedes. He stepped out of the truck even before Jenna managed to. She scrambled to follow, fishing her car keys from her pocket.

There was nothing left to say. It was sad, but it was what it was. And he didn't say anything either, so it was safe to assume that he considered the matter settled.

"Here we are", Chris said. "Hey, I meant it, you know? It was good seeing you again. Good, and a couple other things."

"Yeah", she said. A little awkwardly, she leaned in and gave him a hug. "Bye."

"Drive save", he said.

"Thank you." She clicked her car open.

Chris smiled at her one more time. Then he took two steps backwards to the truck door while saying to her: "And don't let your boss get the better of you during that phone call." He winked and opened the door. She burst out "Chris!" reflexively.

He couldn't have said that for nothing.

Chris held his movement, and she took a step towards him while pulling out the the shirt from under her puffer coat. She held it out to him. Again. "Do you want this?"

He looked at the shirt and then straight into her eyes. "Don't you want it?"

"You were going on about the shirt last night, I just thought that it might be important to you."

He kept his eyes straight on hers. "I just wanted to find out why you were wearing it."

Her phone vibrated in the pocket of her coat. Stanford, for sure. Well, to hell with that bastard.

While losing herself in Chris' eyes, she said, "I still think of you, Chris. Of us. That's what this was about." She teared up and she didn't care that she did. "And I remember why you gave it to me as if it were yesterday", she sniffed and tried to suppress a sob. "On the morning after Bonfire 2004... when I was a total mess because I had smoked pot. I wanted to go home making a good impression on my parents—" Her voice broke but she willed herself to continue. "Not in my... smeared... you know—" She couldn't go on.

Chris had come a step closer, looking at her compassionately. "Of course I know." Chris said and reached for her face, wiping away some tears. She noticed that his eyes were wet as well.

"Jenna... go figure yourself out." he said slowly but determinedly. "And go easy on yourself. You used to believe I was more than I thought I was. Do the same for yourself."

Moving slowly, he opened the door to his truck and

got in. Then the engine started up, and the truck rolled away.

She looked after him and sobs began to shake her. She tumbled into her car, and sat there crying her soul out for minutes and minutes. When Stanford called her again, she picked up only to scream "Fuck off, you disgusting asshole!" She pressed the lumberjack shirt to her chest and waited for the tears to ebb away.

What now?

Jenna gripped the steering wheel and turned on the ignition.

It was a two hour drive to Cincinnati. Plenty of time to change her mind and turn around.

ACKNOWLEDGEMENTS

Initially, all I wanted with *Bonfires* was to record a song. For the first time, though, I had deliberately written the lyrics from a fictional character's point of view. I imagined her life situation, her past, and the other characters she was involved with. This lead me to the idea of sharing more about Jenna and what she experiences on her trip back to her hometown — not just the few lines that she thinks or says in the song.

I've always pursued creative writing in my spare time, but preparing something for publication — especially for the first time — came with many considerations and tasks.

On top of that, my producer Stefan Rebelski had cut such a beautiful piano demo for *Bonfires* that I knew we'd have to record two versions of the song.

In the end, I found myself working on a project that far exceeded my original plan, and involved the support of people whom I am deeply grateful:

MUSIC

Stefan Rebelski: Thank you for breathing life into the song *Bonfires* and turning it into the most beautiful and emotional music!

Eike Ernst and Nils Tuxen: Thank you for contributing your creativity and musicianship to *Bonfires*, especially on those awesome solos!

Anneken Hertzler, who edited the text: A big thank you for all your helpful notes! Your feedback pushed me to go the extra mile, hopefully making *Bonfires* a little bit better.

Linda Nonnewitz, who let me use her amazing acrylic painting *Streets* as the book cover: I can't thank you enough for your generosity! You know I'm a big fan of your art and the beauty you bring into the world through it. Find Linda: www.lindanonnewitz.de | Instagram: lindanonnewitz_art_

Johanna Sänger, my first proofreader: thank you for both your support and your constructive criticism. Both were incredibly helpful.

Jessica Stute, who also proofread, helped me with the layout and put together the book cover: Thank you for supporting this project, especially by designing the fantastic cover. Jessica's Instagram: frollein_jessy_schreibt

Tari Van Noy, my final proofreader: thank you for helping the text cross the finish line!

ABOUT NORA

Nora Sänger has been a singer and songwriter for more than fifteen years. She's released an EP *Transition* (2012), an album *Almost Golden* (2015) and various singles between 2020 - 2022. She loves country and soul music and especially enjoys playing live shows.

Lately, Nora has focused more on her creative writing, something she has done for fun since she was a child. Whenever she can free up some time, she works on a series of stories in her native language, German.

Aside from her artistic endeavors, she works as a vocal coach and choir conductor. She also contributes to her community by organizing cultural events that support local artists.

Nora lives with her husband and their two kids in the Lüneburger Heide region, south of Hamburg.

www.norasanger.com
Instagram: norasangerofficial
get in touch: bonfires@norasaenger.de